RACHEL ISADORA

Babies

Greenwillow Books, New York

Good morning!

Eating

Playing

Laughing

Singing

Dancing

Hugging

Reading

Bathing

Drying

Sleeping

FOR NICHOLAS JAMES MAXIMILLIAN

Library of Congress Cataloging-in-Publication Data
Isadora, Rachel.
Babies/by Rachel Isadora.
p.   cm.
Summary: Babies enjoy the activities of the day, from eating
and dressing up to bathing, drying, and sleeping.
ISBN 0-688-08031-6.   ISBN 0-688-08032-4 (lib. bdg.)
[1. Babies—Fiction.]   I. Title.
PZ7.I763Bab   1989
[E]—dc 19
88-18782   CIP   AC